To Jon & Jamie's dad
-HZ

To my dad, for all the love you gave me
-AH

Text copyright © 2004 by Harriet Ziefert
Illustrations copyright © 2004 by Amanda Haley
All rights reserved. CIP Data is available.
Published in the United States 2004 by
🍎 Blue Apple Books
515 Valley Street, Maplewood, N.J. 07040
www.blueapplebooks.com
Distributed in the U.S. by Chronicle Books
First Edition
Printed in China
ISBN 1-59354-028-0
3 5 7 9 10 8 6 4 2

Harriet Ziefert

33 USES for a DAD

drawings
by
Amanda Haley

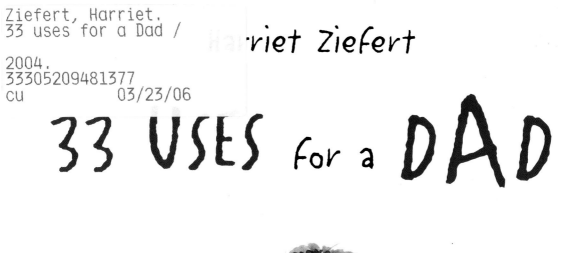

Blue Apple Books

1. nurse

2. dancing partner

3. air conditioner

4. cheerleader

5. opponent

6. ATM machine

7. hand
holder

8. costume designer

9. shopping basket

10. map reader

11. tailor

12. bug
catcher

13. pet feeder

14. alarm clock

15. taxi

16. timekeeper

17. farmer

18. hair stylist

19. swim instructor

20. companion

21. chef

22. coach

23. architect

24. comedian

25. crossing guard

26. horsie

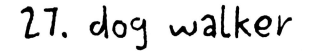

27. dog walker

28.
jar
opener

29. laundress

30.
barber

32. storyteller

33. Friend

THE END

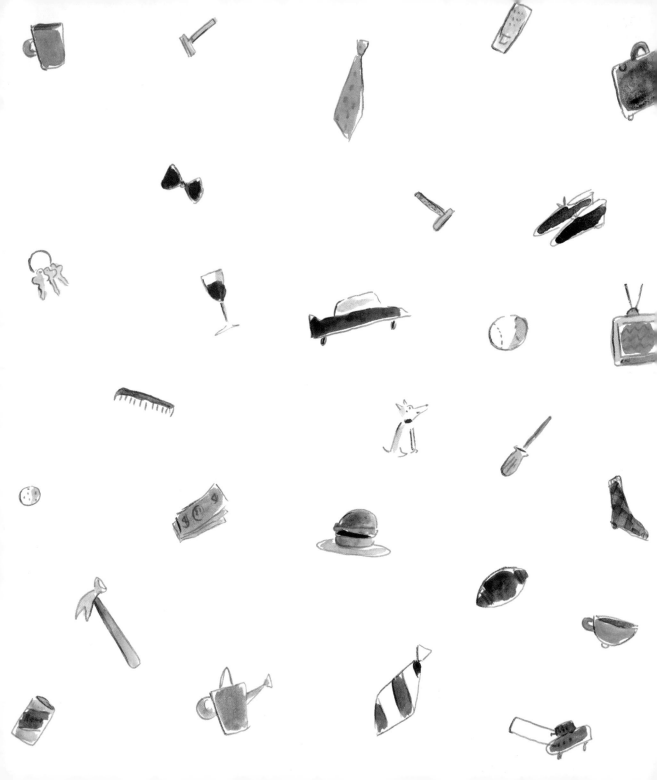

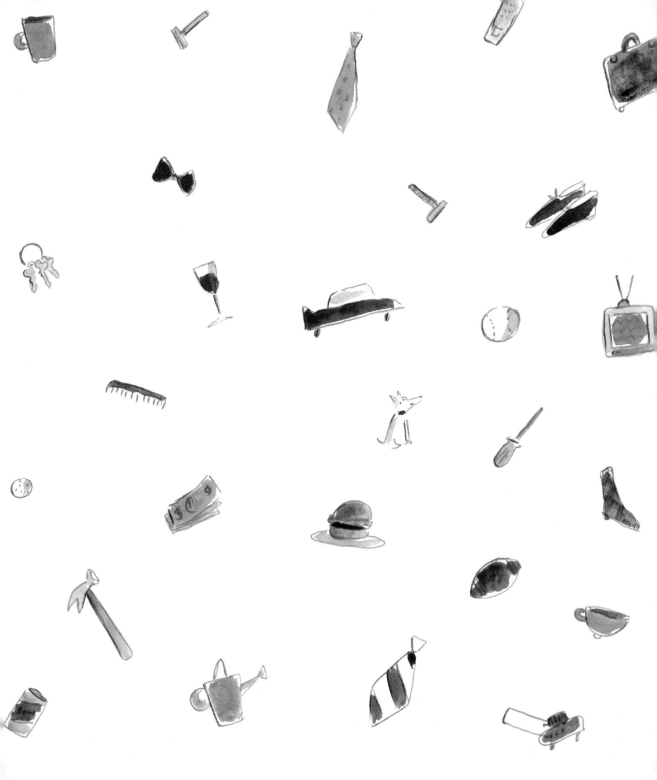